ALAN GARNER'S
Fairytales of Gold

Illustrated by
MICHAEL FOREMAN

Philomel

For Barnaby

Text Copyright © 1979 by Alan Garner
Illustrations Copyright © 1979 by Michael Foreman
First published in England by William Collins Sons & Company, Ltd.,
London and Glasgow. First United States edition 1980,
Philomel Books. Philomel Books are published by The Putnam
Publishing Group, 200 Madison Avenue, New York N.Y. 10016.
Printed in Hong Kong. All rights reserved.
Library of Congress Cataloging in Publication Data
Garner, Alan.
Alan Garner's Fairytales of Gold.
SUMMARY:
Garner, Alan.
Alan Garner's Fairytales of Gold.
CONTENTS: The Princess and the Golden Mane. – The Girl of the Golden Gate. –
The Three Golden Heads of the Well. – The Golden Brothers.
1. Fairytales, English. Children's stories, English. (1. Fairytales)
I. Foreman, Michael 1938- II. Title. III. Title: Fairytales of Gold.
PZ8.G226A1 1980 (Fic) 80-15240
ISBN 0-399-20759-7

CONTENTS

THE
GOLDEN BROTHERS

A poor man and his wife had nothing but a hut. Their only food was fish from the lake. One morning, the poor man cast his net and in it he caught a golden fish, a fish made of gold.

"Throw me back," said the fish. "Throw me back."

"Never," said the poor man. "A golden fish has not been seen in all the world. I shall be rich."

"You are already rich," said the fish. "I have put treasure in your hut. Throw me back."

"What is the use of treasure in a hut?" said the man.

"It is not a hut," said the fish. "I have made you a castle. Throw me back."

"What is the use of treasure and a castle," said the man, "if there is nothing to eat?"

"I have put a cupboard in the castle," said the fish, "and every shelf in the cupboard is filled with food. Throw me back."

"For that," said the man, "I shall throw you back." And he shook the fish out of the net.

"You must never tell," said the fish. "No matter who asks, you must never tell how these things came about. If you do, you will lose all."

So the man went home. And where his hut had stood there was now a castle. His wife came out.

"What has happened?" she said.

"Be quiet," said the man. "Open that cupboard."

And in the cupboard they found cakes, meat, fruit and wine. And they sat down and ate and drank until they were full.

"Where did it come from?" said the wife.

"Don't ask," said the man, "Be thankful."

But his wife was not thankful. Day and night she asked him, until he could stand it no more.

"I caught a golden fish and let it go," he said.

"I don't believe you," said the wife.

"Then look behind you," said the man.

And when the wife looked the castle had gone, and there was only a hut of mud and sticks.

"Go and catch the fish!" she cried.

So the man went to the lake, and cast his net, and when he pulled it in he had caught the golden fish. And everything happened exactly as before, and his wife sent him to cast his net again.

The third time he caught the fish, the fish said, "This is always going to happen, and it is very tiresome. So take me home and cut me into six pieces. Give two pieces to your wife to eat. Give two pieces to your horse. Put two pieces in the ground."

The man did all these things. And the
two pieces of the fish that he put in the
ground became two golden lilies. The
horse bore two golden foals. The wife bore
two golden boys, alike as mirrors.

Boys, foals and lilies grew. And one day the two brothers said that they wanted to ride out on their golden horses into the world.

"How shall your mother and I know that you are well?" said the father.

"The golden lilies will remain," said the brothers. "If they are well, we shall be well. If they fade, we shall be sick. If they die, we shall be dead." And they rode away into the world.

Everywhere the brothers went the people laughed at them. No one had ever seen boys made of gold.

One of the brothers was shy, and he
turned back and went home to his parents.
But the other was bold and angry, and he
went on.

And he came to a forest that was full of robbers. He thought that if he went in there both he and his horse would be killed for the gold that made them.

So he caught a bear and skinned it, and covered himself and the horse with raw fur, and he entered the forest. The robbers moved all around him, but he rode on.

"Who's that?" said a voice.
"Kill him," said another.
"Leave him," said another voice. "He has only a raw bearskin that stinks."
So the golden boy came safe through that forest.

Beyond the forest there was a village, and in it was the most beautiful girl in the world alive. As soon as he saw her, the boy loved her.

"Marry me," said the boy.
"I will," said the girl.
So the girl and the golden boy were married, and lived happily.

But one day the boy woke, and said to the girl, "I dreamt I was hunting and rode a great stag. I must find that stag, wherever it may be in the world, for my heart will not rest."

"I am afraid," said the girl. "We are so happy here, you and I. Do not go into the world again for anyone or anything."

"I must go," said the boy. "If I do not find that great stag, my heart will die."

"Stay," said the girl. "Stay, and be happy."

"I cannot stay," said the golden boy. "I cannot be happy. I dreamt I rode a great stag."

"It was a dream," said the girl. "Only a dream."

"Then I must find a dream," said the golden boy. And he left the girl weeping.

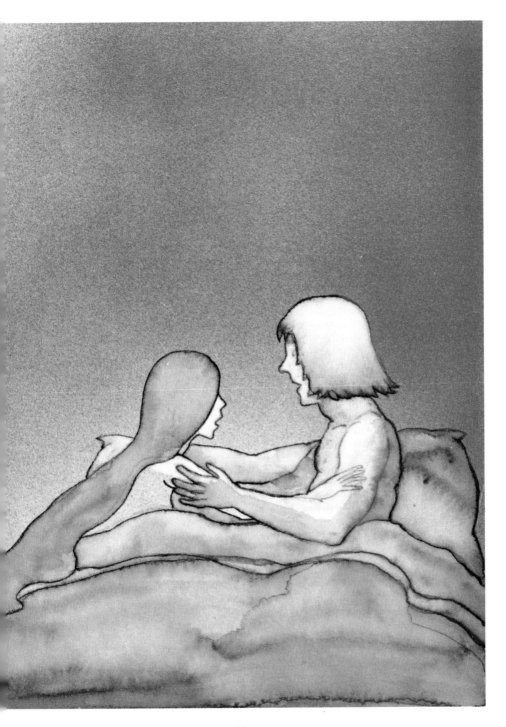

He came to a forest, and in a glade deep
in that forest was the stag. It was waiting for
him. And when the boy saw it, the stag
trotted away, leading him on and on
through the forest and through the world,

through nights and days and dreams and
waking, until, at evening, it disappeared.

The boy was tired, but he looked around to find the stag, and he saw a cottage in a wood. He knocked on the door, and an old witch opened it.

"Do you know a great stag?" said the golden boy. "I have lost it."

"Yes," said the witch. "I know that stag. Come in."

The boy went into the cottage, and the witch turned him to stone.

But back at the castle, where the father and mother and the second golden boy all lived content together, out of the world's laughter, one of the two golden lilies snapped.

"Something has happened to my brother," said the second golden boy. "I must help him."

And he rode back again into the world and over it until he came to the witch's cottage in the wood.

"Have you my brother?" he said to the witch.

"Yes," said the witch. "And he is stone. But he is a better man than you. For he risks himself in life, while you sit by, out of the world, at home."

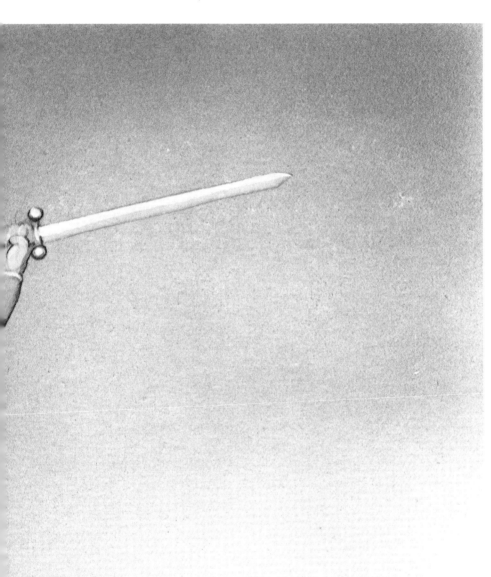

But the brother drew his sword and took
the witch by the hair. "Give me back my
brother!" he said.

And the witch was afraid, and she turned the stone boy back to gold, and the two golden brothers were together, alike as mirrors.

Together they rode awhile, and then they parted. One went back to the village of the most beautiful girl of the world, and one to their father and mother.

And in the castle,
whole again,
the golden lilies grew.

THE GIRL OF
THE GOLDEN GATE

A man and his wife had only one child, and she was a girl. The mother didn't like the girl and made her do all the hard work in the house, and she beat her and sent her to bed hungry each night.

One day, the mother thought she would be rid of the girl altogether, so she told her to go on an errand across three fields. The fields were bewitched, and the mother knew that the girl would be killed.

And the girl went on the errand.

When she came to the first field she saw
that it was covered with fire, and she stood
still at the edge and dared not cross it. But
she was afraid to go back home, because she
knew her mother would beat her.

She could not go back, she could not go on, so she tried to go around the field. But the field was bewitched, and instead of going around it, the girl came to a wall. There was a door in the wall, and the girl opened it and went through into a wood.

She walked for a long time through the
wood, and it was very dark, without sun or
moon. At last she saw the light of a house and
she knocked at the door.

A fox opened the door.

"What do you want?" said the fox.

"I am tired and hungry and have nowhere to go," said the girl.

"If I let you come in, you must be my maid for a year," said the fox.

"Will you beat me?" said the girl.

"Beat you I shall not do," said the fox.

"Will you feed me and clothe me?" said the girl.

"Feed you and clothe you I shall do," said the fox.

So the girl went in, and the fox fed her and clothed her, and did not beat her, and she worked for him.

Every morning the fox went out early, and every evening he came back late. But the girl was happy in the house, and kept it clean and bright.

One day the fox said, "I am going on a journey. While I am gone, there are five things you must not do. You must not wash the dishes. You must not sweep the floor. You must not dust the chairs. You must not open the cupboard. And you must not look under my bed."

"I shall not," said the girl.

And away went the fox.

The girl sat in the house and wondered why the fox had told her not to do the five things. And after she had sat and wondered she could think of nothing else.

"I'll see what happens," she said. "One won't hurt."

So the girl washed all the dishes in the house, and as soon as she had finished, a great bag full of copper fell down before her out of the air.

"Very good," said the girl. "One more won't hurt."

So she swept the floor, and as soon as she had finished, down fell a bag full of silver.

"Better yet," said the girl. "One more won't hurt."

She dusted the chairs, and as soon as she had finished, down fell a bag full of gold.

"Best of all," said the girl. "One more won't hurt."

The girl went to the cupboard and opened it. The cupboard was big and black, and all that was in it was a gold ring.

"That's pretty," said the girl. And she put the ring on her finger.

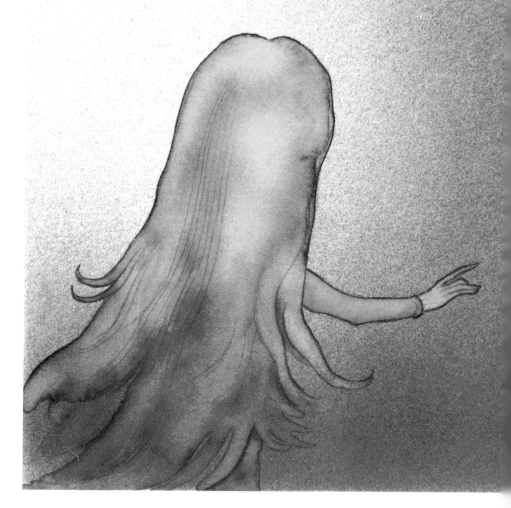

As soon as the ring was on her finger, the girl heard a noise, and a golden ball bounced down the stairs.

"Oh, you don't know how glad I am!" said the girl, and she picked up the golden ball and put it in her pocket.

The girl climbed the stairs to the fox's bedroom, and looked under the bed. And there was the fox.

The girl ran down the stairs, past the fox's cat, out of the house, past the fox's cow, along the garden path, past the fox's mule, through the gate, past the fox's dog, and into the wood, past an owl in an oak. And she ran and she ran.

The fox came down the stairs, and said to
the cat,
   "Cat of mine, cat of mine,
   "Have you met a maid of mine?"
   And the cat said, "She has just passed by."
   The fox went out of the house, and said to
the cow,
   "Cow of mine, cow of mine,
   "Have you met a maid of mine?"
   And the cow said, "She has just passed by."

The fox went along the garden path, and
said to the mule,
   "*Mule of mine, mule of mine,*
   "*Have you met a maid of mine?*"
And the mule said, "She has just passed
by."

The fox went through the gate, and
said to the dog,
   "*Dog of mine, dog of mine,*
   "*Have you met a maid of mine?*"
And the dog said, "She has just passed
by."

Last of all, the fox said to the owl in the oak,

"*Owl of mine, owl of mine,*

"*Have you met a maid of mine?*"

And the owl said, "She has just passed by."

"Which way did she go?" said the fox.

And the owl said, "Over the stream, and across the ditch, and behind the wood you shall find her."

Away ran the fox, over the stream, and across the ditch, and behind the wood after the girl, to find her.

And the girl ran and she ran, and she heard the fox coming behind her.

She ran and she ran until the wood
ended. In front of her were three fields.
When she reached the first field it was
covered with fire, and she saw her own
house, and her mother watching from the
window. And behind her she heard the fox.

The fire was so hot that she put her hands over her face. And the ring jumped from her finger and rolled into the fire. And, where it rolled, a path followed it across the field, and the girl ran along the path to the other side.

And the fox ran after her down the path. But when the girl reached the other side the path disappeared, and the fox was burnt up, and all the fire went through the middle of the ring and melted it, so that ring, fox and fire were gone.

The mother came out of the house and
said, "Give me the golden ball."

But the girl would not. She hurried to the
second field. And the field grew covered
with water and the girl could not get across.

The girl was so afraid that she dropped
the ball into the water. The ball floated.
And the mother came nearer and nearer.

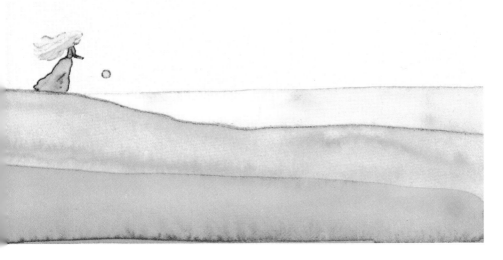

So the girl stepped onto the golden ball, and it carried her across the water to the other side of the second field, and she stood on dry land.

The mother was swimming to catch the girl. But the golden ball floated away over the world, and the water followed it, and the mother was drowned.

The third field was green grass and red flowers. And in the middle was a gate of gold, alone, tall with arches and pillars, wrought of gold.

And the girl walked into the field and
through the golden gate.
And no one saw her
again.

THE THREE
GOLDEN HEADS OF
THE WELL

Once upon a time, and a very good time it was, though it wasn't in my time, nor in your time, nor in anyone else's time, there was a king and a queen. And the king had a daughter, and the queen had a daughter. And the king's daughter was bonny and good-natured, and everybody liked her. But the queen's daughter was ugly and ill-natured, and nobody liked her.

And the queen didn't like the king's daughter, and she wanted her away. So she gave her a sieve, and she said, "Go to the Well of the World's End, and bring me home the sieve full of water to drink."

The queen thought the girl would never find the Well of the World's End, and even if she did, she would never fill a sieve.

So the girl went and she went, and she asked everywhere for the Well of the World's End. But nobody knew.

She came to a moorland and to a pony
that was tethered with a rope to a tree. And
the pony said to her,
"*Flit me, flit me, my bonny May,*
"*For I haven't been flitted*
"*For seven years and a day.*"

And the king's daughter said, "Yes, I shall, my bonny pony. I'll flit you." And she did. And the pony gave her a ride over the Moor of Hecklepins.

Now, she left the pony, and went on, far and far and more than I can say, until she did come to the Well of the World's End. But what must she do with the sieve?

The well was deep, and she dipped and
dipped, but no water could she lift.

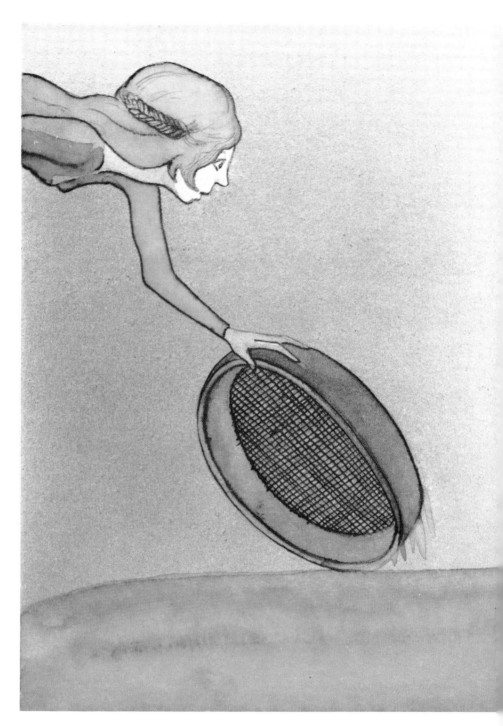

Then she saw rising up through the water of the Well of the World's End the golden head of man. And the head spoke to her.

"Wash me, wash me, my bonny May,
"And lay me on a primrose bank to dry."

"Yes, I shall, my bonny head," said the king's daughter. "I'll wash you." And so she did.

And another golden head rose up
through the water, and said,
  "Wash me, wash me, my bonny May,
  "And dry me with clean linen, pray."

"Yes, I shall, my bonny head," said the king's daughter. "I'll wash you." And so she did.

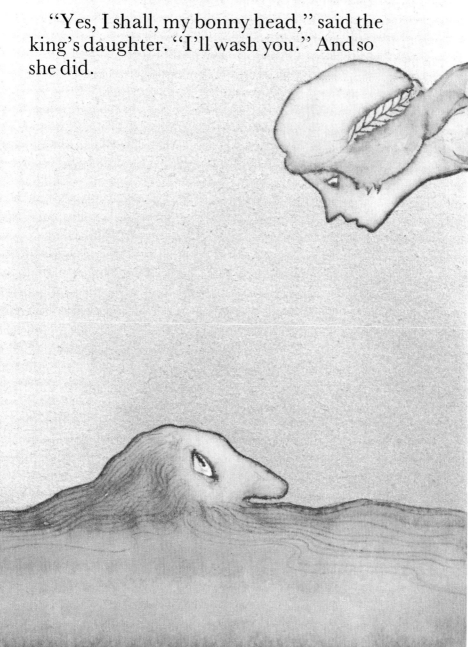

And a third head of gold rose through the water of the Well of the World's End. And it said,

"*Wash me, and comb me,*
"*And lay me down softly,*
"*And lay me on a primrose bank to dry,*
"*That I may look pretty,*
"*When people pass by.*"

"Yes, I shall, my bonny head," said the king's daughter. "I'll wash you." And so she did.

And the three heads together began to
sink into the water of the Well of the
World's End, and the water faded the gold
to yellow.

The heads spoke one to the other.

"Say, brother, say, what do you say?"

And the first said, "I say that if she was
bonny before, she'll be bonnier yet."

"Say, brother, say, what do you say?"
The water turned yellow to green.
And the second said, "I say that every
time she speaks, a diamond and a ruby
and a pearl shall drop from her mouth."

The water turned green to blue.

"Say, brother, say, what do you say?"

And the third said, "I say that every time she combs her hair, she'll get a peck of gold and a peck of silver out of it."

"But how shall I carry my sieve full of water away?" said the king's daughter.

A diamond and a ruby and a pearl
dropped from her mouth when she spoke,
and they rippled the water till she could no
longer see the three golden heads in the
dark of the Well of the World's End. But she
heard their voices.

"Stop it with moss, and daub it with clay,
"And then it will carry the water away."

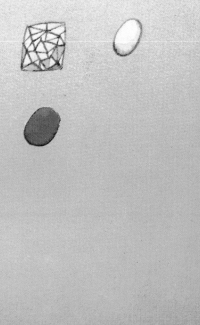

So the king's daughter took some moss
and lined the sieve with it. Then she
smoothed clay over all the moss and
dipped the sieve in the well, and not a drop
was lost.

And so she came back to the palace and
gave the sieve of water to the queen.

And if the king's daughter was bonny before, she was bonnier now. And every time that she opened her lips to speak, a diamond and a ruby and a pearl dropped from her mouth. And every time that she combed her hair, she got a peck of gold and a peck of silver out of it. And she married a prince.

The queen was vexed, and she didn't know what to do; but she thought she would send her own daughter to see if she could fall in with the same luck. So she gave her daughter a glass bottle and sent her to fetch water from the Well of the World's End.

The queen's daughter went and she went, and she asked everywhere for the Well of the World's End. But nobody knew.

She came to a moorland and to a pony
that was tethered with a rope to a tree. And
the pony said to her,
"*Flit me, flit me, my bonny May,*
"*For I haven't been flitted*
"*For seven years and a day.*"
And the queen's daughter said, "You
nasty beast, do you think I'll flit you? I'm a
queen's daughter!"

So she wouldn't loose the pony, and the pony wouldn't give her a ride over the Moor of Hecklepins. She had to go in her bare feet, and the hecklepins cut and pricked her till she could hardly walk.

Now, she went far and far and more than I can say, until she did come to the Well of the World's End. And she sat on the edge of the well and bathed her feet in the water.

And a golden head rose through the water of the Well of the World's End and said to her,

"*Wash me, wash me, my bonny May,*
"*And lay me on a primrose bank to dry.*"

"Wash you, you round bobbing beast?" she said. "I'm a queen's daughter!" And she pushed the head away with her foot.

And a second golden head rose up
through the water of the Well of the
World's End, and said,
  "Wash me, wash me, my bonny May,
  "And dry me with clean linen, pray."
  "I'm washing myself," said the queen's
daughter.

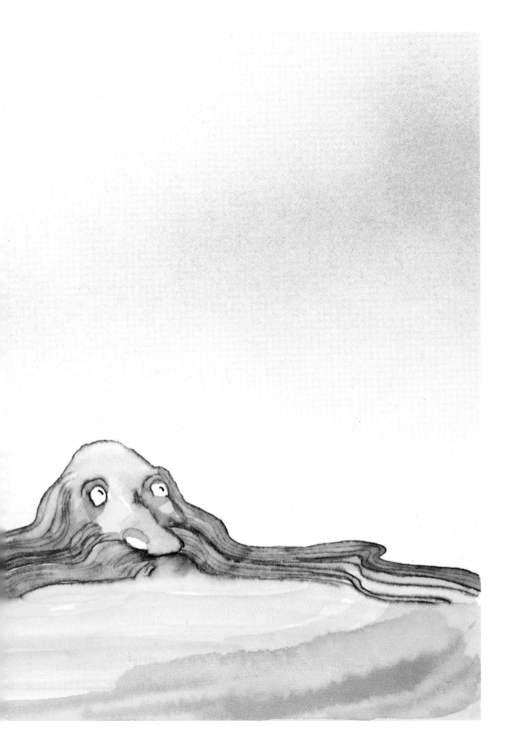

And a third golden head came, and it said,
"Wash me, and comb me,
"And lay me down softly,
"And lay me on a primrose bank to dry,
"That I may look pretty,
"When people pass by."

"You, look pretty?" she said. "Take that for your washing!" And the queen's daughter hit the golden head with her bottle.

The three golden heads sank into the water of the Well of the World's End, and water faded the gold to yellow.

The heads spoke one to the other.
"Say, brother, say, what do you say?"
And the first said, "I say that if she was
ugly before, she'll be uglier yet."

The water turned yellow to green.
"Say, brother, say, what do you say?"
And the second said, "I say that every
time she speaks, a toad and a yellow-
bellied asker shall drop from her mouth."

The water turned green to blue.
"Say, brother, say, what do you say?"
And the third said, "I say that every
time she combs her hair, she'll get a peck of
fleas out of it, and for marrying she'll have
to put up with an old cobbler."

The queen's daughter dipped her bottle
in the water of the Well of the World's End.
But though the bottle was made of glass,
the water ran through it as if it were a sieve.
And however she tried, she couldn't take up
the water, not at all.

"But how shall I carry my bottle away?"
she cried.

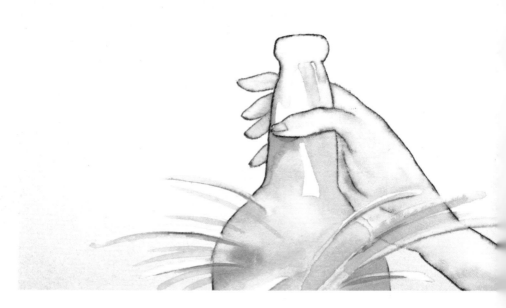

And as she spoke, a toad and a yellow-bellied asker dropped from her mouth, and she could no longer see the three golden heads of the Well of the World's End. But she heard their voices.

"*Stop it with fog,*
"*And daub it with mist,*
"*And get you the husband*
"*You'd never have kissed!*"

The queen's daughter went away home, over the Moor of Hecklepins, and her bottle stayed empty.

And when she told her story, every time
she opened her lips a toad and a yellow-
bellied asker dropped from her mouth,
until her mother forbade her to speak.

So she went to her room, weeping, and combed her hair. And every time she combed it, she got a peck of fleas, until the king said he would pay anyone to marry her if only he could be rid of her. And if she was ugly before, she was uglier now, but an old cobbler said that he would have her.

So the queen's daughter was married to the old cobbler, and he leathered her with a strap every day. And that's all.

THE PRINCESS
AND
THE GOLDEN MANE

A king had a daughter, but was jealous of her beauty, and would not let her marry. So she fell in love with a stableboy of the palace, and he loved her as much as she loved him, and they were married secretly.

After a while, the stableboy came to the princess and said, "I must go away, or your father will have me killed. You will bear two children, a boy and a girl. Look after them. If you or they are ever in danger, tell the white horse with the golden mane."

Then the princess wept, and kissed her husband, and he went away. But, before he left, he asked the palace blacksmith to put three bands of iron about his heart, so that it would not break. And when that was done, the stableboy set out to find some place that would be safe from the power of the king.

The princess bore two children, boy and girl. And her father was so angry that he sent messengers and soldiers through all the world to find the stableboy who had married his princess.

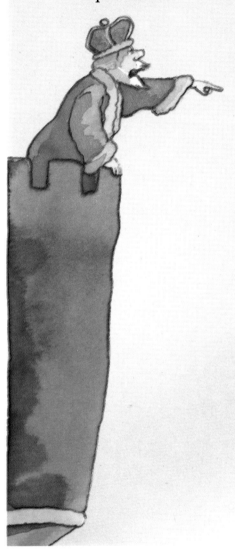

But the messengers and the soldiers
came back and said that they could not find
him in any kingdom on earth or under it.

"Then look beyond kingdoms," said the
king. "Look in the deserts and the
mountains. Look in the oceans and the
stars. But find him. He must be found."

The messengers and the soldiers went out again, and looked beyond kingdoms, in the deserts and the mountains, in the oceans and the stars. But they did not find him. They came back and said, "He is not anywhere to be found. He must be dead."

The king raged that his revenge was lost: and the princess mourned her husband. Yet the king was still angry. He took a flea and fed it until it was as big and as fat as an ox. Then he skinned the flea, and said that any man who could tell what animal it was that owned such a skin would earn the king's daughter for nothing.

Many came, but none could tell what animal owned such a skin. At last, an old beggarman said, "It is the skin of a flea."

So the king gave the princess to the old beggarman, and told her to make ready to go with him.

The princess went to the stable and looked for the white horse with a golden mane, and when she found it she said, "My husband is lost, and I am given to an old beggarman, and I fear for my children."

The white horse said, "Ask your father to let you take a horse for you and your children on the journey."

"He will not let me, and the beggarman will not want the children," said the princess.

"The king may not let you, but the beggarman will want the children," said the horse.

So the princess went back to the king, and she said, "Father, I am ready. But let me take a horse for the journey, for me and my children."

"You will take nothing," said the king, "and the children will stay."

"I want the children," said the beggarman.

"Then take them," said the king, "and the horse."

The princess mounted the white horse with her children, and the beggarman held the bridle and led them off.

They travelled without stopping, without speaking. The children laid their heads on the golden mane, and slept. And the tears of the princess were frozen.

They came at last to a great castle on a rock, and entered the courtyard. The beggarman took the princess and her children into a room where there was a table laid with every good thing to eat and drink, and he watched them while they ate, but he himself did not taste the food, nor did he speak. Then the princess put the children to bed, and the beggarman went from the room.

"Follow him, follow him," the horse called to the princess.

So the princess followed the beggarman
through the castle. And as the beggarman
walked, he grew bigger, until he reached a
cave in the rock beneath the castle, where a
fire burned under a cooking pot, and in the
light of the fire the princess saw that the
beggarman was an ogre and the cave was
filled with bones.

The ogre dipped his hands into the pot,
and ate.

The princess ran back and told the horse
what she had seen.

"Wake the children and come," said the
horse.

The princess woke the children, and they
left the castle and mounted the white horse
with the golden mane.

The horse galloped off into the night.

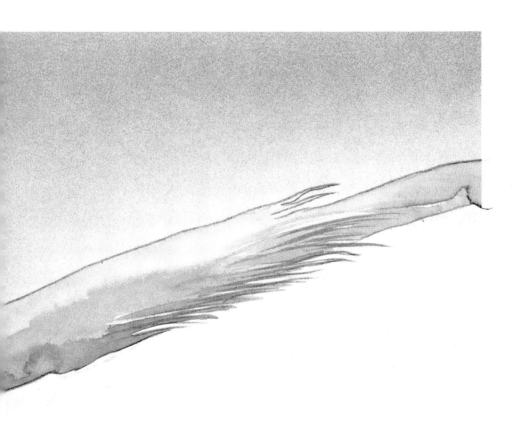

Far below, in the cave in the rock, the ogre heard the hooves ringing, and he roared and came out of the castle and his eyes smoked up like torches, and he saw the white horse riding.

"More to a meal than ears and thumbs," said the ogre, and he set off to catch the children and the princess.

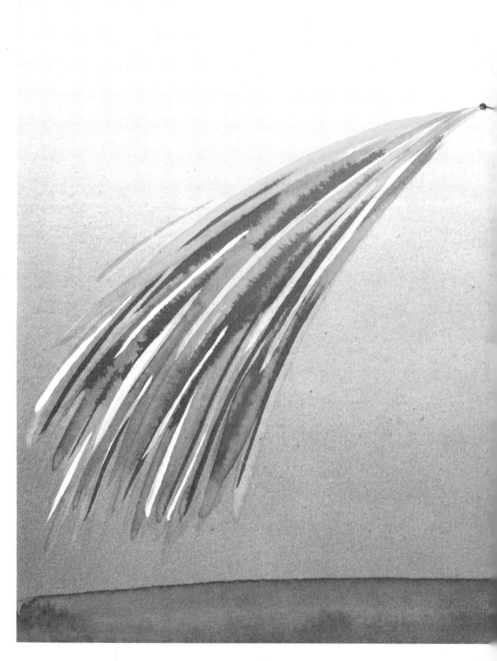

The horse galloped fast, but the ogre's arms stretched out and grew and grew, until the fingers snatched a hair from the horse's tail.

The horse said, "In my mane you will find a rose. Throw it behind us."

The princess put her hand into the golden mane and pulled out a golden rose, and she threw it behind her. The rose became a waterfall of fire in the sky, and the ogre had to stop.

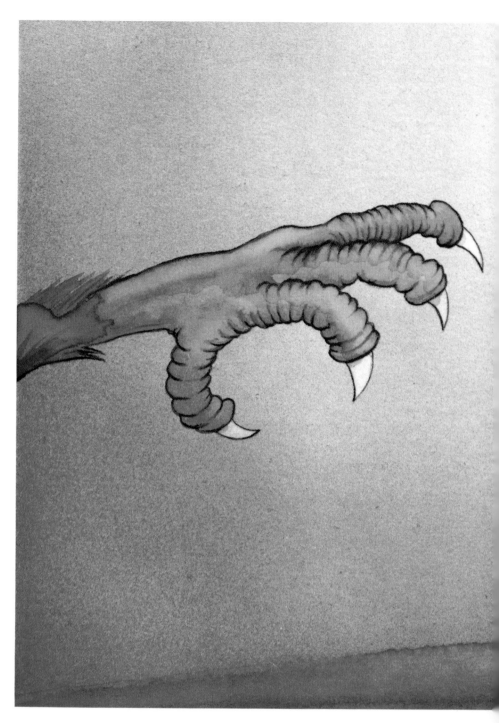

But he came on again, so close that
he snatched two hairs from the horse's tail,
and said, "More to a meal than ears and
thumbs."

The horse said, "In my mane you will find
a peck of salt. Throw it behind us."

The princess put her hand into the golden
mane and pulled out a peck of salt, and she
threw it behind her.

The salt turned into a mountain of glass which the ogre could not climb, though the sound of his claws shivered the wind. He had to go round the mountain.

"More to a meal than ears and thumbs," said the ogre, and soon he had caught up with the horse, near enough to snatch three hairs from its tail.

The horse said, "In my mane you will find a comb. Throw it behind us."

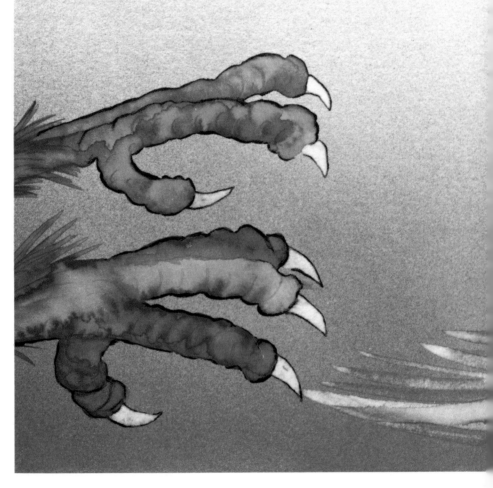

The princess put her hand into the golden mane and pulled out a golden comb, and she threw it behind her.

The comb turned into a forest of bronze, all briar and thorn of bronze, and the ogre could not pass through. He had to go round the forest.

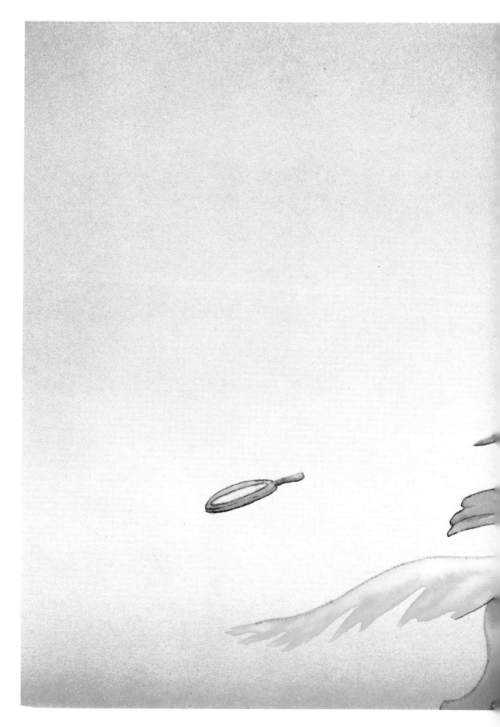

"More to a meal than ears and thumbs,"
said the ogre.

The horse said, "I am tired. We are at
the desert of the end of the world. In my
mane you will find a mirror. Throw it
behind us."

The princess put her hand into the golden
mane and pulled out a golden mirror, and
she threw it behind her.

The mirror turned into a lake that lay like a sea. The horse was on one side of the lake, the ogre on the other.

"How shall I get across?" said the ogre.

"Tie a stone to your neck, and swim," said the princess.

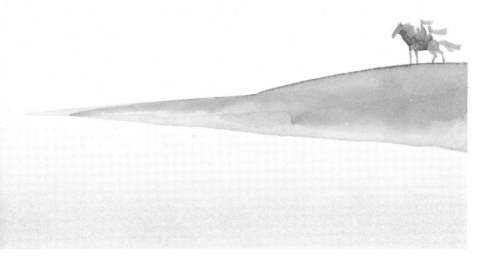

The ogre took the biggest stone of the desert and tied it around his neck and jumped into the water. And still he swam.

"More to a meal than ears and thumbs," said the ogre.

The horse said to the princess, "Get down. There is nowhere else to run."

So the princess held her children, and the horse went into the lake, and horse and ogre both disappeared. But the water boiled and steamed red with their fighting.

And they fought for so long, so hard, that the lake was dry. And where the lake had been was the horse. And the ogre was dead.

The horse said, "Now you must do exactly as I tell you. You must kill me. You must throw my ribs towards the sun, my head towards the moon, and my legs to the four horizons of the sky."

"How can I kill you when you have saved our lives?" said the princess.

The horse said, "Do it."

So the princess killed the horse. She threw its ribs towards the sun, its head towards the moon, and its legs to the four horizons of the sky.

And the legs were four gold poplar trees
with emerald leaves, and from under the
ribs came villages and fields and meadows,
flowing over the desert of the end of the
world, and the ribs were a golden castle.
And out of the head came a river of silver
water, and on the river was a boat, and in
the boat was the stableboy.

And so the princess found her husband, and the children their father, and the stableboy took the iron from his heart. And they lived long together in that green and golden land.